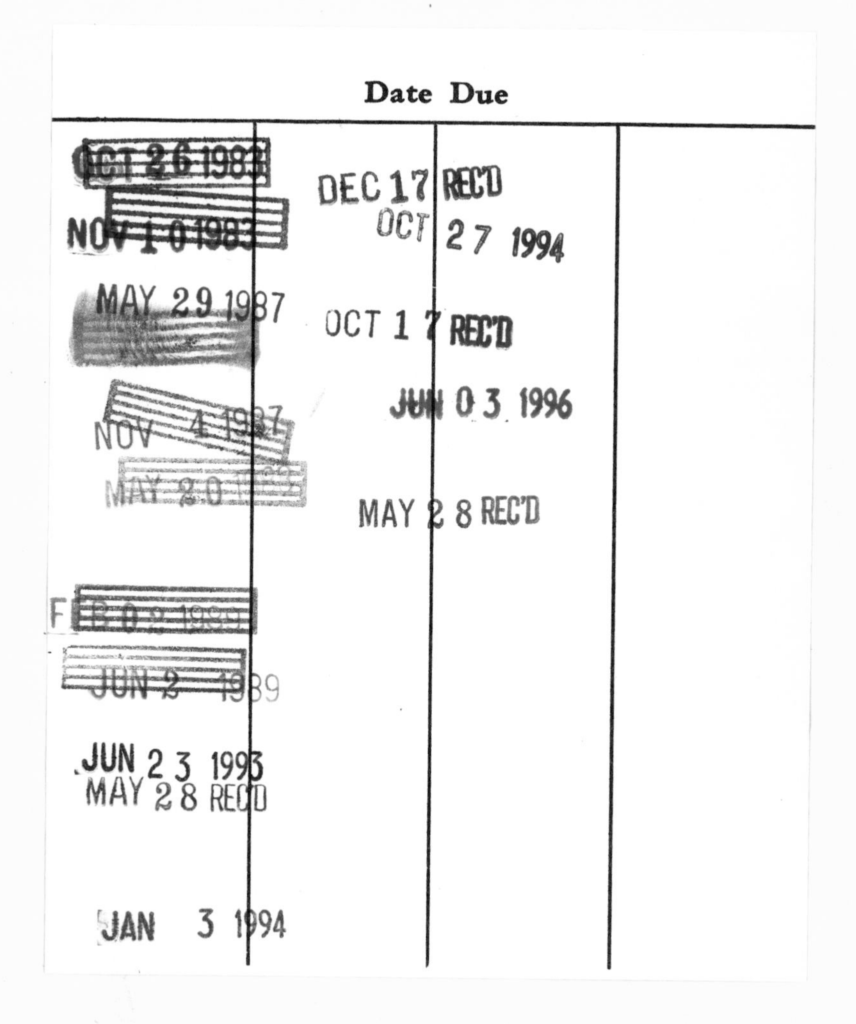
Date Due
OCT 26 1983
NOV 10 1983
MAY 29 1987
NOV 4 1987
MAY 20
FEB 02 1989
JUN 2 1989
JUN 23 1993
MAY 28 REC'D
JAN 3 1994
DEC 17 REC'D
OCT 27 1994
OCT 17 REC'D
JUN 03 1996
MAY 28 REC'D

MILLICENT THE MAGNIFICENT

MILLICENT THE MAGNIFICENT

by Alice Bach

Pictures by Steven Kellogg

Harper and Row, Publishers
New York, Hagerstown, San Francisco, London

Millicent the Magnificent

 Printed in the United States of America. For information address Harper & Row, Publishers, Inc., 10 East 53rd Street, New York, N. Y. 10022. Published simultaneously in Canada by Fitzhenry & Whiteside Limited, Toronto.

FIRST EDITION

Library of Congress Cataloging in Publication Data
Bach, Alice.
Millicent the Magnificent.

SUMMARY: When Oliver becomes a pupil of Millicent, a circus bear, his brother Ronald decides to secretly teach himself the same tricks.
[1. Bears—Fiction. 2. Twins—Fiction.
3. Acrobats and acrobatics—Fiction] I. Kellogg, Steven. II. Title.
PZ7.B1314Mi [E] 77-11840
ISBN 0-06-020309-9
ISBN 0-06-020312-9 lib. bdg.

For Maudie and Mae

mothering bears

Oliver tugged at the rope he had tied around the trunk of the chestnut tree. "C'mon, big fella, easy boy."

"You call all trees *boy*?"

Oliver turned around and saw a girl bear about his size. "I was practicing—it's my horse and I'm a rodeo trainer." He wished she would stop laughing.

"Rodeo, huh. Can you leap onto the back of a cantering pony?" Oliver frowned. "There are no real ponies in this wood."

She cartwheeled until she was standing next to Oliver. "I'm Millicent, Girl Wonder. I hurtle through the air faster than any bear."

"You sure are faster than any bear! I'm Oliver."

"Rodeo bear?"

"Not a real rodeo. It's a game."

"What is your act?"

Oliver had to lie down and twist upside down to look at Millicent, who was standing on her head. "I don't have one. You have an act?"

"You bet your billboard. I've worked two shows daily since I was a baby. Come one, come all, to Mr. Wuffiluff's Family Circus. All-live animal acts. Thrills and chills for all you Jacks and Jills."

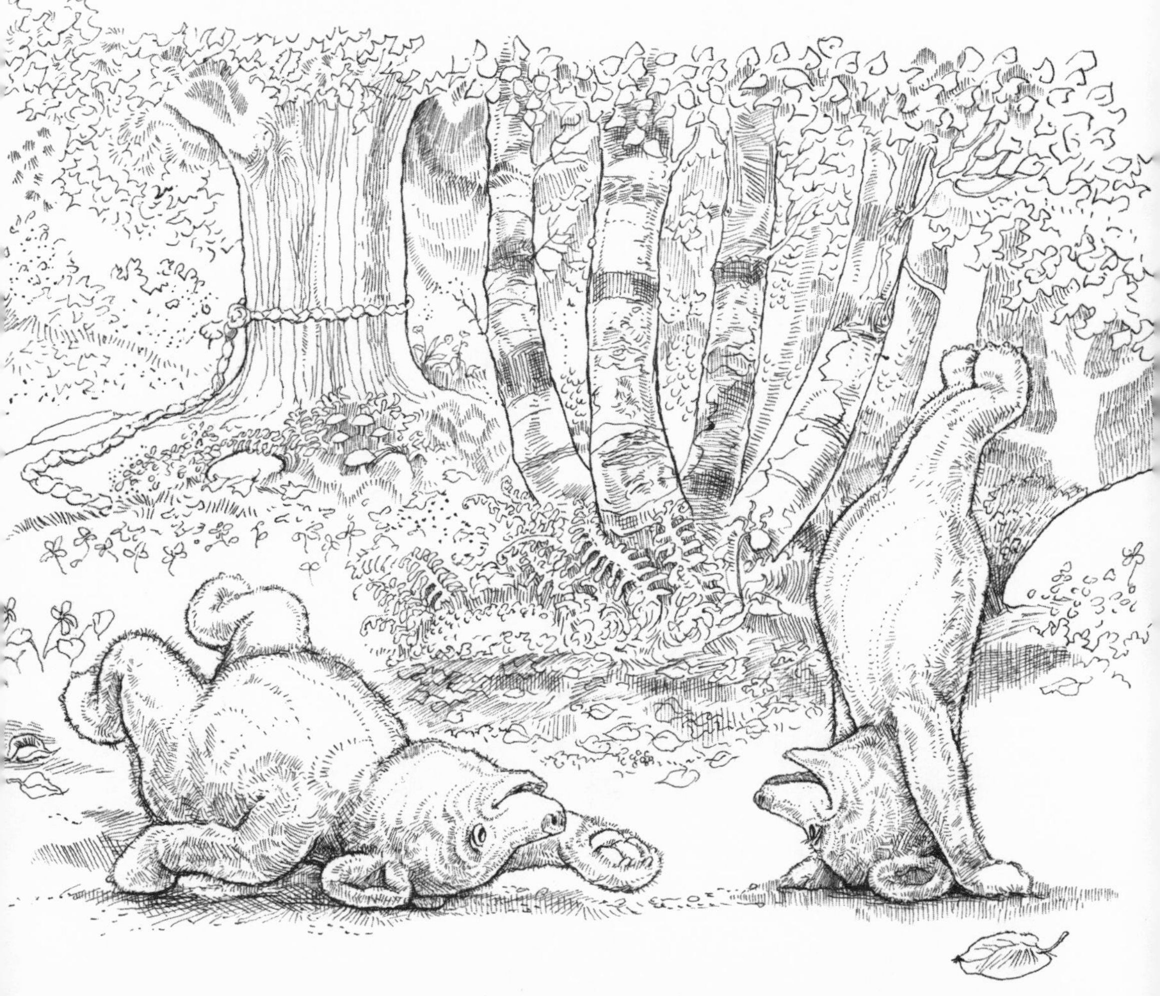

"You're really a circus bear?" Oliver inched across the ground to keep pace with Millicent, who was ambling along on her hands. She nodded. "Might as well go back to taming your tree if all you can do is gape like I'm Madame Jocasta, the Two-headed Woman."

"I'm sorry, Millicent. I never met a circus bear."

"I figured. My old man is Sir Sampson, the best unicyclist in the world."

"Is the circus coming here? Will Sir Sampson do his tricks?"

"Not a chance. He quit Mr. Wuffiluff's. That's why we're here."

"How come he quit?"

"They wanted him to carry one of the clowns on his shoulders during the grand parade. It happened once before. We left and Mr. Wuffiluff begged my old man to come back. Since he is the best—"

"What do you call *that* trick?"

"A double back flip with a split finish." Millicent walked backward on her hands until she had made a circle around Oliver. "It's been nice talking to you. You're the first bear I've talked to since we made camp. Anyway I'd better make tracks. If I don't help pitch the tent I'll be sidelined for a week."

"Pitch the tent?"

"Oliver, if you ask one more question, it will be 'How come Millicent, Girl Wonder, disappeared so fast?' *Get me?*"

"You bet. Will you come by our cabin tomorrow?" Oliver clapped his paw over his mouth. "Pretend it wasn't a question, OK?"

"I'll drop by in the A.M. Might be fun. A performer's life is lonely. I never live anywhere long enough to have friends."

"I'm your friend. And wait 'til you meet my twin. Ronald. He's the smartest bear in the world."

"Has he traveled all over the world?"

"Of course not. We've always lived in a cabin on the north side of the wood."

"Then he's the smartest bear in the wood, not the world."

"Better not let Ronald hear you say that."

"Millicent the Magnificent can take care of herself."

"Then you'll come."

"Sure. If you've got any talent, we can block out a simple routine."

Oliver ran home. "Ma, I met this girl bear, she's going to teach me and Ronald in the morning."

"Teach me what?" Ronald put a chocolate cookie in his book to mark the place.

"An act, a routine. She walks on her hands."

"Feet suit me fine for walking."

"Please, Ronald. There's nothing to do." Oliver snatched the cookie from Ronald's book and gulped it. "I hate playing alone."

Ma brushed the crumbs from Oliver's chest. "Play outside with Oliver until dinner-time, Ronald."

"Let's play geography." Ronald tucked his book under his arm and kicked at a pile of leaves outside the door.

"I always lose."

Ronald twirled the rope around the tree. "You're not still playing giddyap horsey, are you?"

"So what if I was? Millicent's going to teach us circus tricks. Maybe someday we'll be bareback riders in the circus."

"Go play with her. This bear is not interested."

"Then you can't take any more books out of the library on my card. And I'm telling Pa you pretend to be sick to get out of gym."

"OK, I'll be the lion tamer. You be the lion." Ronald picked up a stick. Oliver crouched on all fours and growled ferociously.

"Go to sleep, lion. Sleep." Ronald waved the stick. Oliver roared a few times and yawned. He pawed the ground and lay down at Ronald's feet.

"Now I can read how to wake up lions." Ronald stretched out under the tree and opened his book.

"I hate you." Oliver jumped up. "You'll be sorry when Millicent and I are famous and you're home alone reading a book."

"Stop whining. You're no circus bear."

"Wait and see."

Oliver had been watching for Millicent since dawn. He couldn't wait to get started. "Hey, Millicent." He waved. "Ronald's not interested in walking on his hands."

"What's his problem?"

"Circuses aren't serious enough for him."

"Circuses aren't serious? Rehearsal every day to clean up your act? Perfecting new routines? Working even when you've got a fierce cold and your eyes are runny? Where is this jive bear? Let him make fun of the circus to my face."

Oliver grabbed Millicent's paw and ran back to the cabin. Millicent might be the only bear who could talk faster than Ronald.

"Ma, this is my friend Millicent." Ma stepped back as Millicent smiled and did two back flips. "Ronald here?"

"In his room, Oliver. Where is your family building their cabin?"

"We're tenting. We travel light. Pop hauls the tent, his cycle, extra inner tubes, air pump, tools. Ma carries bowls, a couple pots, and her special pillow. I'm in charge of Sir Sampson's costumes and rain gear."

"He says he'll come in when he finishes the chapter." Oliver smiled at Millicent.

"You got a balance beam?" Millicent looked around. "What a jerk question. I forget not everyone's a circus bear. We've never lived anywhere more than two weeks."

"Our Festival is in three weeks. Maybe your father would ride—"

"I'm sorry, ma'am. Not a chance. His only freebie is the Silent Cycles benefit once a year."

"Silent cycle?" Ronald crossed the kitchen glaring at Millicent.

OTTO
REFRIGERATION

"You must be Ron. Silent Cycles are the gents who've ridden for the last time. No more performances 'til the big circus in the sky."

"Old bears who've lost their balance?" Ronald sneered.

"Watch it, Ron. I'm a trained magician."

"Magic is illusion. Sleight of hand."

"You're pushing, buster." Millicent stood on her head and edged her right paw close to Ronald. As he bent to grab it, she flipped upright, socking him in the chin. "Sleight of foot."

Oliver applauded. "Ma, did you see that?"

"You asked for it, Ronald. I must go to Aunt Bear's. We're the entertainment committee for Festival."

"Don't bet a button on my old man. His policy is money up front. Then the act."

"Why don't *we* do something for Festival?" Oliver put his arm around Millicent.

Millicent nodded. "We might work up a simple routine. I'll do the flashy tricks and you can be my assistants." Ma tied her bonnet and left.

"I'm nobody's assistant," Ronald snapped.

"Fine, you be the ringer."

"What's a ringer?" Oliver asked.

"The one who talks the stragglers into the tent." She scowled at Ronald. "I think you'd be perfect for that slot, Mr. Mouth."

"All you know is tricks. I could learn them before nightfall."

"OK, turkey, come outside."

Millicent paced up and down. Finally she motioned to Ronald. "Ground's flat here." She did three forward flips and leaped up to catch a low branch.

"Somersaults is all." Ronald crouched and flipped over—flat on his back. He lay quite still, chewing his lip.

"Rock back before you tuck your head. You need more momentum. Try again." Millicent hugged her branch.

Ronald groaned, lifted his head off the ground, and fell back.

Millicent applauded and whistled. "You're sure a showstopper, Ron. You'll be headlining in a couple days."

"Shut up," Ronald growled. He twitched and moaned. "OOHHHHH."

"What hurts?" Oliver ran to his brother. "Are you OK?"

"I fell against this root." Ronald sat up slowly and slid a few inches closer to the root. "My back is bruised. I'd better knock off."

"So much for his career," said Millicent. "No place for cupcakes in the circus. Performers get used to bruises."

"I don't give a fig for flops and flips. Let's see how much you know." Ronald tapped his head. "Between the ears. How does a refrigerator work?"

Millicent climbed higher in the tree. "Refrigerator? OK, sweetheart. Inside a refrigerator live polar bears. Very small polar bears. They work in the back of the fridge, that's why you hear humming. They're happy bears. They push the ice into all the corners with their long snouts."

"Just in case anyone asks you, it works with electricity and compressed air."

"I may not know about compressed air, but I recognize hot air when I hear it."

"You don't know rocks from clocks," Ronald said, but he did not look happy.

"Oliver, today we concentrate on the basic headstand. Care to run through it with us, Ron?"

"If you weren't a girl . . ."

"You'd what, lock me in a refrigerator?"

"We'll see the best act—at Festival."

"Ronald, please stay." Oliver said. "It'll be more fun."

"You want to learn tricks with boastful Bertha, that's your choice."

Millicent smiled at Oliver. "Ready? Spread your front paws about this far apart. Now kneel and drop your head down on your chest." Oliver imitated Millicent and rolled over on his back. "Try again," she said crisply. Five tries later Oliver said, "I guess I'm as bad as Ronald. Some bears can't do circus tricks."

Millicent brushed the twigs off his back. "Don't be like him. He's not so great. He just says he is."

"I'll never be a circus bear."

"I know it's hard. You can come to the tent and watch when Sir Sampson's teaching me a new trick. I fall and groan, and sometimes I even cry."

"You're so tough. There's no trick you couldn't learn."

"I'll tell you a secret. I'll never work the trapeze. It scares me silly. Your timing goes off by a second and you're on your way to the ground."

"You think I could ever be good enough to do an act with you, maybe even join the circus?"

"I'll teach you everything I know. If we were a team, I'd never get lonely between shows."

"And I won't have to play rodeo by myself!"

"My cousin Natalie sweated three years before she could work the high wire without a net. We'll have to practice all the time. We have to want it a lot."

Oliver nodded. "I want it a lot."

They practiced all morning. Oliver thought his head must be getting flat as the ground. He wasn't even hungry.

Millicent stood behind him repeating *again* 'til Oliver wished he had never heard of the circus. When the sun had fallen behind the trees, and he could barely see Millicent, Oliver got so mad, he kicked his legs into the air.

"Straighten your back," Millicent said in the flat tone that made Oliver feel like a no-talent jerk.

"Let go of my legs. Let me do it myself." She stepped back and Oliver stayed straight as a candle, balancing on his head and front paws.

"Millicent! I love it! I'm never coming down!"

"You've got the balance now. You'll be able to stand on your head whenever you want. Let's pack it in for today."

Oliver sat on the ground, grinning. Then he spread his front paws, kicked up, and straightened tall. He waved his hind paws. "We're going to have an act," he yelled. "Oliver, Circus Bear!"

"Tomorrow we start hard work," Millicent said. "I hope you don't change your mind,

chicken out." She sighed. "It would be nice to have a partner. Millicent the Magnificent and Oliver."

"I'm in for keeps. I can do a headstand. I can learn anything."

"You can tell Mr. Bragging Bear that this is only the beginning. By Festival we'll be wearing spangled costumes. We'll have an act sharp enough for the center ring."

Oliver skipped home calling over his shoulder, "See you in the A.M."

Oliver saluted Ronald and did a headstand.

"That's wonderful. Millicent must be a good teacher," Pa said and motioned Oliver to sit at the table.

"A couple stunts is all she can do." Ronald stared at his plate.

"You couldn't even do a somersault. Turkey!"

"Oliver!"

"Sorry, Ma. But he thinks he knows everything."

"So she can flip around like a fish and climb trees like a squirrel. Big deal."

Oliver stood on his head next to Ronald's chair. "Care to say that upside down?"

"Boys, one more cross word and you'll both go to bed immediately after supper."

"Millicent's mother is going to make us real circus costumes," Oliver said.

Lying in the dark, Ronald mapped out his plan. "I'll get a book on acrobatics. By Festival I'll outcircus that show-off bear. Nobody's going to make fun of this bear. I bet she thinks tiny bears build campfires inside the stove, hot enough to cook our food. I'll show you, Millicent, *sweetheart.*"

During the next two weeks Oliver left the house after a quick breakfast and came home a minute before supper. He ached. His arm muscles were killing him, he could barely straighten his back. His head throbbed as though he were still whirling through the air. Even his ears felt floppy.

He'd cartwheel the last few steps home. Ma and Pa were amazed at how fast he had caught on. He could walk on his hands, do double flips, backward and forward, almost as fast as Millicent. They were going to practice to music, to give their act a professional touch—they would outshine all the bears at Festival.

BEAR

Ronald said nothing. He kept his door shut. Aside from a few thumps and moans no one saw or heard him all day. Ronald ached too. But he couldn't complain. Because then they'd know that he was practicing, that he was desperate to be as good an acrobat as Millicent, to prove he was still the greatest bear in the wood. He could do anything.

The problem was he couldn't hurtle through the air—at all. Why he ached was simple. He kept losing his balance. Too many times he had kicked up with his feet, wavered, and slammed down thump on his nose.

He studied the diagrams in the acrobat book. He tried the hint for headstands: "While practicing the headstand, place your head a few inches from the wall and kick straight up. The wall will prevent you from flopping on your face."

Ronald's wall did save his nose. But there would be no wall at Festival. Each time Ronald moved away from the wall, he landed on his sore nose. He shuddered at the thought of trying to walk on his front paws. It hurt to walk right side up. He had memorized the book but the words were no help. Festival was two days off.

Ronald prayed for rain.

"Hotcakes, Oliver?" Ma asked.

"Just a pair, Ma. Got to be a streamlined bear if I'm going to make it to center ring."

Ronald's head sank onto his chest. He pretended to read the book on his lap, but he was watching his brother, wishing Oliver would stumble or fall. But Oliver didn't miss a beat.

"How's your act, Ron baby?"

"Call me Ron baby again and I'll show you my act!" Ronald shook his paw in Oliver's face.

"Ronald, you've been snappish the past few days. Is something wrong?" Pa leaned across the table.

Ronald shook his head. "May I be excused?" He looked defiantly at Oliver.

"Pa and I have to leave to set up the booths," Ma said. "You boys come over when you're ready."

"Mill is coming over as soon as her old lady sews on our spangles for our crowns," he smiled at Ronald.

"Does he have to talk about Millicent and his dumb costume all the time?" Ronald screamed.

“Let’s take a walk, son.” Pa wiped his mouth and laid his napkin on the table.

“I don’t want to take a walk,” Ronald muttered, but he followed Pa outside.

"Having a problem with your act?"

"Of course not. I can do anything I put my mind to."

"Oliver's found talent he didn't know he had with this circus business."

Ronald fell on the ground. His muscles were so sore he couldn't walk another step.

"Your act giving you trouble?"

"I have memorized the book." Ronald started to cry. Pa sat down and put his arm around him. "I know what I'm supposed to do, Pa, but my arms and legs won't do it."

"I see."

"They're going to laugh at me, worst of all that creep with her hotshot spangled costume. She makes me sick."

"Millicent's grown up in the circus. A performer's life–"

"I know. But she brags all the time. She thinks she's just the best bear ever."

"Do you know any other cubs who brag a lot?" Pa hugged Ronald.

"Maybe I have. Once or twice." He waved his paws wildly. "She's going to make fun of me."

"I'm surprised such a smart bear not knowing his own act."

"Who wants to be in a two-bit circus?"

"Apparently you do."

He rubbed his face against Pa's warm chest.

"Oliver is a super acrobat. That doesn't mean Ronald should snap, or mope, or fall until his nose swells up." Pa kissed Ronald's head and gently patted his puffy nose. "It's Oliver's turn to shine today."

Ronald massaged his sore neck. He would return the acrobat book to the library. He'd never have to look at it again. "Will you and Ma sit with me during their act?"

"Of course. You know, they might need someone who knows how to talk loud and swell to introduce their act." Pa stood up and smiled. "I'll save you a seat between Ma and me."

Millicent and Oliver were walking toward him. Ronald took a deep breath and scratched his leg. "You both look very big-time," he said softly.

"There may be scouts here to catch our act. In a few years we will be center ring. The toast of six continents," Millicent said.

Oliver swirled his cape. "We're going to be stars."

Ronald cleared his throat. "Ladies and Gentlemen, come one, come all, to witness stupefying daredevil tricks. Thrill to the stars Millicent the Magnificent and the One and Only Oliver. You haven't seen the big time until you watch this pair." Ronald paused and cleared his throat. Then he yelled at the top of his voice: "They hurtle through the air faster than any bear."

"You bellowed that better than Rudolpho, and he's been ringmaster for Mr. Wuffiluff since before I was born."

"Would you consider, Ronald, just for today, would you be our Rudolpho? Please?" Oliver hoisted Millicent onto his shoulders.

Millicent adjusted her crown. "C'mon, Ron, sweetheart, help us make Festival as big-time as the circus."

"Certainly. I planned it all along. I know my own act."